Charlie Cook's Favourite Book has also been used as part of an exciting interactive exhibition that started at Discover Children's Story Centre in London before moving to the Z-arts centre in Manchester. For the entrance to the exhibition, the designers made a real-life version of Charlie Cook's living room, complete with his favourite cosy chair – just right for curling up in with a good book. They even had some special fabric with the pattern of parrots and flowers from Axel's illustration in the book, to make it look just right.

Here is a picture of Axel and me, and the real-life chair based on the one in *Charlie Cook's Favourite Book*.

And now it's been fifteen years since Charlie first curled up in his chair to read his favourite book. So I'd better say many happy returns to the pirate, Sir Percy Pilkington, Rowena Reddalot and all the rest of the characters – and, of course, most of all to Charlie Cook himself!

Julia Donaldson

Julia Donaldson has written a song based on *Charlie Cook's Favourite Book*. It's called 'A World Inside a Book', and you can find it inside another book called *A Treasury of Songs*.

For Alice, Alison and Alyx

First published 2005 by Macmillan Children's Books
This edition published 2020 by Macmillan Children's Books
an imprint of Pan Macmillan
The Smithson, 6 Briset Street, London EC1M 5NR
Associated companies throughout the world
www.panmacmillan.com

ISBN: 978-1-5290-2346-6

1 3 5 7 9 8 6 4 2

A CIP catalogue record for this book is available from the British Library.

Printed in China.

WRITTEN BY
JULIA DONALDSON

ILLUSTRATED BY
AXEL SCHEFFLER

Charlie Cook's Favourite Book

MACMILLAN CHILDREN'S BOOKS

Once upon a time there was a boy
called Charlie Cook
Who curled up in a cosy chair
and read his favourite book . . .

About a leaky pirate ship
which very nearly sank
And a pirate chief who got the blame
and had to walk the plank.
The chief swam to an island
and went digging with his hook.

At last he found a treasure chest,
and in it was a book . . .

About a girl called Goldilocks,
and three indignant bears
Who cried, "Who's had our porridge?
Who's been sitting on our chairs?"

They went into the bedroom,
and Baby Bear said, "Look!
She's in my bed, and what is more,
she's got my favourite book . . ."

AS HE READ ALOUD A JOKE HE'D FOUND (INSIDE HIS FAVOURITE BOOK)...

About Rowena Reddalot,
a very well-read frog,

Who jumped upon a lily pad

and jumped upon a log,

Then jumped into the library
which stood beside the brook,

 And went, "Reddit! Reddit! Reddit!"
as she jumped upon a book...

About an oak tree full of birds.
Each bird had built a nest
And they had a competition
to decide which one was best.

They chose an owl to judge it,
and the winner was a rook
Whose nest was lined with pages
from his very favourite book . . .

About a girl who saw

a flying saucer in the sky.

Some small green men were in it

and they waved as they flew by.

She tugged her mother's sleeve and said,

"Look, Mum, what I've just seen!"

But Mum said, "Hush, I'm trying to read

my favourite magazine . . ."

About a wicked jewel thief who stole the King's best crown

**But then got stuck
behind some sheep,
which slowed his
car right down.**

**The King dialled 999
and soon the cops
had caught the crook,**

**And flung him into prison,
where he read his favourite book ...**

About a greedy crocodile

who got fed up with fish

And went on land to try to find

some other kind of dish.

He went into a bookshop
and he there grew even greedier

While reading (on page 90
of a large encyclopedia) . . .

CAKE: a mixture of nice things, usually baked in the oven. It is eaten at teatime and on special occasions like birthdays and Christmas.

THE QUEEN'S BIRTHDAY CAKE

It took six lorries to carry the Cocoa Munchies for the Queen's birthday cake to the palace. The cake also required 4,276 bars of chocolate and 739 sackfuls of marshmallows. The special outsize cake tin was made by the Royal Blacksmith, using 2,647 melted-down horseshoes.

FAMOUS CAKE-EATERS

Britain's most famous cake-eaters are the Bunn twins of York. At the age of six they became the youngest ever winners of the York Festival Cake-Eating Competition. Aged ten, they had to be taken to hospital after knocking each other out, while both reaching for the same slice of cake. (Their dog then ate the cake.)

About the biggest birthday cake the world had ever seen. A team of royal cakemakers had made it for the Queen.

The cake was so delicious
     that a famous spaceman took
A slice of it to Jupiter.
     He also took a book . . .

About a ghost who glided
round a castle every night,

Carrying her head and
giving everyone a fright.

She kept it up till morning,
then she found a shady nook

And put her head back on again
to read her favourite book...

About a cosy armchair,
and a boy called Charlie Cook.

Drawing Charlie Cook

Charlie Cook's Favourite Book is unusual because it hasn't really got one continuous story but jumps from story to story. When I first read Julia's text and started to think about the illustrations, I wanted all the stories in Charlie's book to look different from one another. I thought I might use a different style to draw each one. But in the end there wasn't enough time to work it all out. And maybe that was a good thing – it would have been very tricky!

But I did draw lots of different versions of all the pictures to decide how each of them should look. And some of them changed along the way.

Here are some of the early sketches that I drew for the pages about Goldilocks and the three bears. Can you see what changed at each stage?

I painted the final picture more than once too. How many differences can you spot?

Can you find the page with the final picture in this book? Is it different again?